Christmas
ACTIVITY

This book belongs to:

_____

_____

First published by Parragon in 2013
Parragon
Chartist House
15–17 Trim Street
Bath BA1 1HA, UK
www.parragon.com

Copyright © Parragon Books Ltd 2013

Written by Ben Hubbard   Illustrated by Steve Wood
Edited by Robyn Newton   Designed by Kathryn Davies
Production by Richard Wheeler

ISBN 978-1-4723-2064-3

Printed in China

Christmas
ACTIVITY

PaRragon

Bath · New York · Singapore · Hong Kong · Cologne · Delhi
Melbourne · Amsterdam · Johannesburg · Shenzhen

He's Here!

Color Santa so he is ready to deliver the presents.

Jingle Bells

How many bells can you count on this horse and sleigh?

Jingle bells, jingle bells, jingle all the way ...

Christmas Tree Pairs

Draw lines to connect the matching decorations, then color in the tree!

Market Madness

How many Santa lookalikes can you find at this Christmas market?

Joke

Q: What goes "Oh, oh, oh"?
A: Santa walking backwards.

Answer: 10 Santas

Sketch a Snowman

1 Draw two round snow circles for a body.

2 Add sticks for arms.

3 Draw a hat on its head.

4 Add a carrot for a nose and dots for the eyes and mouth.

Now create a few more friendly snowmen!

Snowflake Search

All snowflakes are different, but not on this page!
Can you find the matching pair?

JOKE

Q: Why is it always
cold at Christmas?
A: Because
Christmas is in
Decemberrrrrr!

Ready, Set, Search!

Santa is running late! Help him collect his sleigh and his nine reindeer, so he can deliver the presents on time.

START

Joke

Q: Where do you find reindeer?
A: Wherever you left them!

FINISH

Beautiful Branches

Deck the tree with lots more of your own decorations!

Design-a-Reindeer

Give each reindeer a different look.

Squeeeeeeeze!

Which fireplace will Santa
reach with his big sack of presents?

a

b

c

Pretty Paper

Add color and patterns to these perfectly wrapped presents.

Penguin Pick-out

Can you spot eight differences between these two snowy scenes?

Delicious Thanksgiving Dinner

Add food to every plate on the table — make it look as yummy as you can!

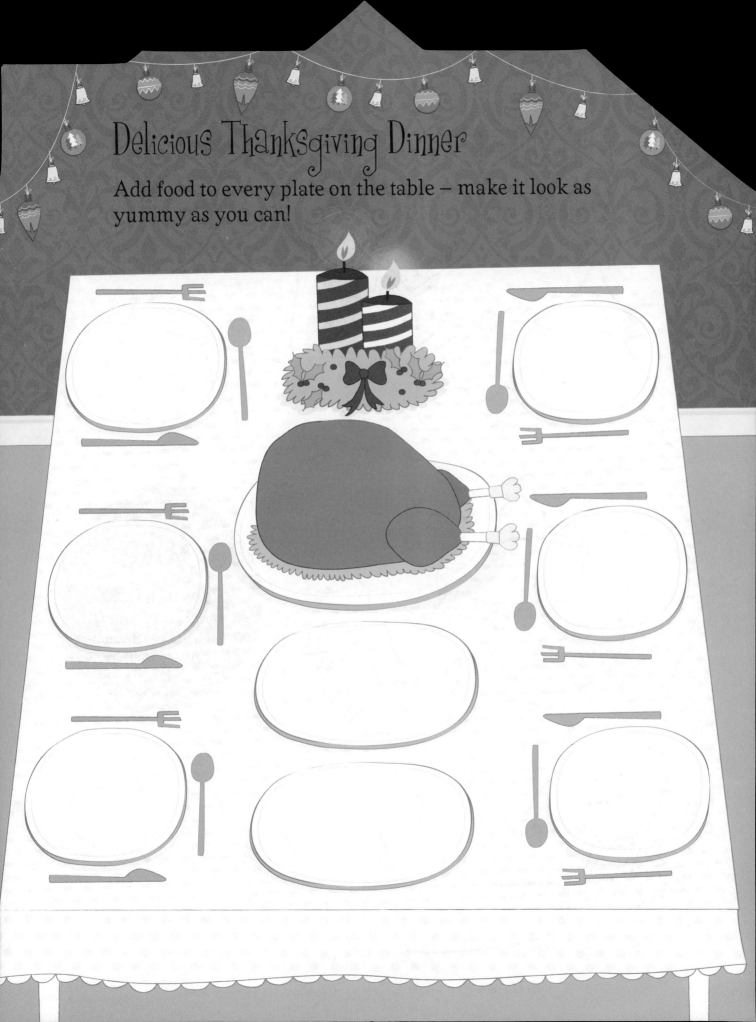

Christmas Chaos

Color and count every Christmas shape you can see.
Which shapes do not belong here?

Joke

Q: Why are Xmas trees bad at knitting?
A: They keep dropping their needles!

Surprise!

What is this lucky little girl
getting for Christmas?

Jolly Gingerbread Men!

These gingerbread men are loose in Santa's village.
Can you find and circle them all?

Joke

Q: What does a gingerbread man with a sore leg need?

A: A candy cane!

NORTH POLE

Present Pile Up

There are lots of brightly colored presents under the tree. How many of each color are there? Write your answers in the empty boxes below.

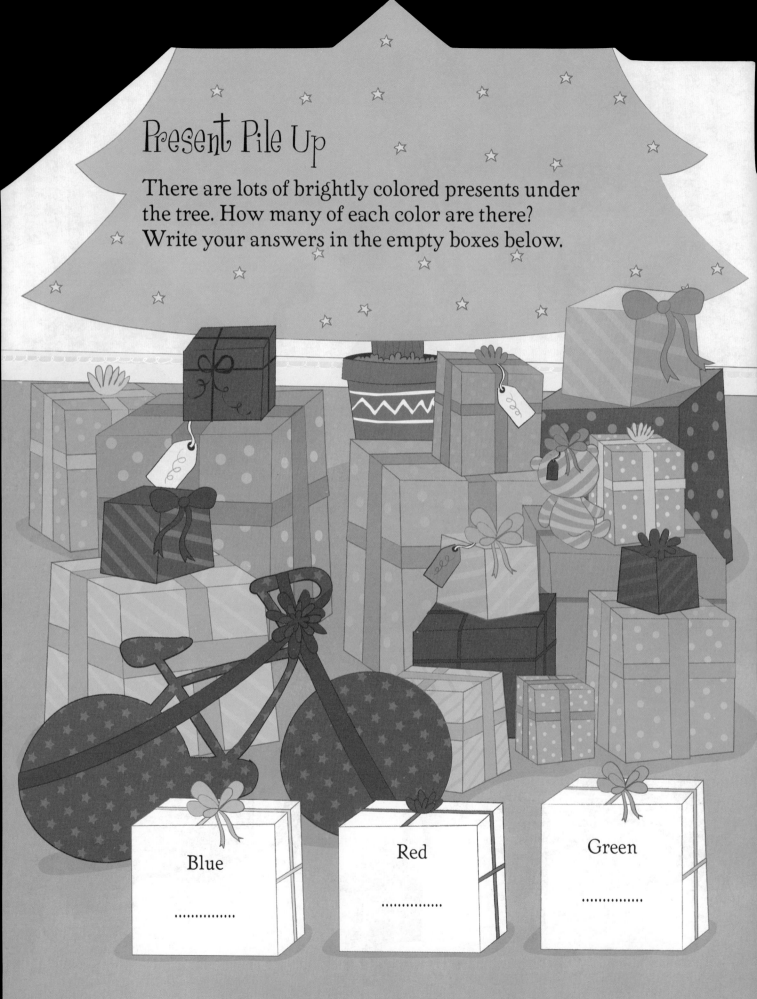

Blue

....

Red

....

Green

....

Which One?

These silly animals all want to be Santa's reindeer.
But can you find the real one?

Who Took Santa's Snack?

Which line of crumbs leads to the cookie cruncher?

Answer: The dog

Reindeer Squares

Draw a reindeer!
Copy one square at a time
to become an expert!

Light the Way

Add the correct shapes to finish off
these crazy Christmas light patterns.

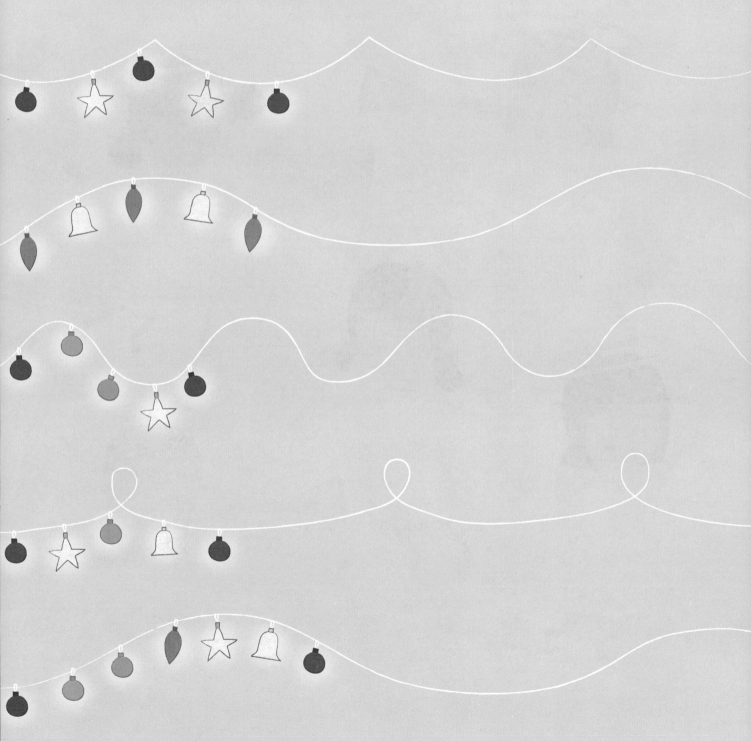

Angel Artwork

Some of these Christmas angels are missing something.
Fill in the missing wings, halos, and trumpets.

Christmas Crash!

Santa's sleigh has fallen into a tree and there are presents everywhere! Find and color each one.

Who delivers Christmas presents to dogs?

Santa Paws!

We almost Forgot about Christmas!

Give this room a magical Christmas makeover.
Add color to the tree, then add lots of presents,
stockings, and plenty of decorations.

Christmas Treats

Can you find the treat that does not belong in each row?

Who's Pulling the Sleigh Today?

Connect the dots and color it in to find out!

I wonder when my reindeer will get back from vacation?

Match the Footprints

Follow the lines to match each animal to its footprints.

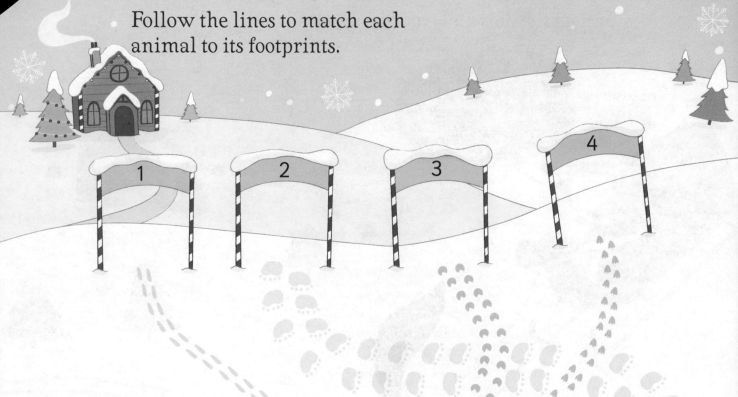

Elf Yourself!

Draw and color a friendly elf face for each little helper!

Joke

Q: What's the first thing that elves learn at school?
A: The elf-abet.

Half the Fun!

Draw the other halves to complete these Christmas friends.

Stocking Surprise!

What is inside each colorful stocking?
Draw a line to match each stocking with the present inside it.

Nativity I-Spy

Can you find everything in this nativity scene?

Circle each one you find in the main picture.

3 wise men

3 shepherds

3 sheep

1 angel

1 big star

1 baby Jesus

Workshop Search

How many busy elves can you find
and color in Santa's workshop?

Christmas Carolers

Can you find the six singers
who don't fit in?

Deck the halls with cats and cobwebs.

Color Crazy!
Make Elf Town colorful and Christmassy.

ELF TOWN

Dear Santa ...

Draw the things you'd like for
Christmas on this wish list.

For Christmas this year I'd like ...

Up and Up!

This trunk is definitely missing something!
Add a big and beautiful Christmas tree to
fill the space!

Signs in the Sky

Connect the stars in the sky to create a
Christmas cartoon. Who will it be?

Wishing you a ...

Trace the letters to make this Christmas
message clear, then finish coloring the picture!

Merry
Christmas